As I stared at the words stitched on the needlepoint pillow, my cheeks burned. Leave it to my mother to transform Christmas morning into an Embarrass-Nori-Fest. Since arriving back in Ten Commandments, Iowa two days ago, I'd put up with non-stop innuendos, commentary, and sermons about my living-in-sin lifestyle and ticking biological clock. However, with the gift I'd just opened, Mom had gone too far. Way too far.

Acclaim for *Talk Gertie to Me*

"Whimsical, funny, and original, Winston's small-town-girl-makes-good romance shouldn't be missed." – *Booklist*

"One of the most outrageously funny, heart-warming stories you will ever read." – *The Romance Readers Connection*

"Totally delightful, laugh-out-loud funny book that leaves the reader wanting more." – *Fresh Fiction*

"...One of the most unique, enjoyable, and hilarious stories I have ever read." – Romance Junkies
Reader

"Laughter, wit and just a touch of womanly wisdom give (*Talk Gertie to Me*) a fresh take." – eBookIsle.com

"Talk Gertie to Me scores with fast-paced, witty dialogue and loveable characters! Lois Winston crafts sparkling humor and simply hilarious encounters between the sexes, all while weaving in a great contemporary romance..." – 5 Angels, Fallen Angel Reviews

"A fun book that I didn't want to put down." – Gotta Write Network

"Absolutely hilarious!!" – 5 stars, Huntress Reviews

"You have to read this. It's a blast!" – Novel Talk Reviews

Books by Lois Winston

Anastasia Pollack Crafting Mystery series
Assault with a Deadly Glue Gun
Death by Killer Mop Doll
Revenge of the Crafty Corpse
Decoupage Can Be Deadly
A Stitch to Die For
Scrapbook of Murder
Drop Dead Ornaments
Handmade Ho-Ho Homicide
A Sew Deadly Cruise
Stitch, Bake, Die!
Guilty as Framed
A Crafty Collage of Crime
Sorry, Knot Sorry

Anastasia Pollack Crafting Mini-Mysteries
Crewel Intentions
Mosaic Mayhem
Patchwork Peril
Crafty Crimes (all 3 novellas in one volume)

Empty Nest Mystery Series
Definitely Dead
Literally Dead

Romantic Suspense
Love, Lies and a Double Shot of Deception
Lost in Manhattan
Someone to Watch Over Me

Romance and Chick Lit
Talk Gertie to Me
Four Uncles and a Wedding
Hooking Mr. Right
Finding Hope

Novellas and Novelettes
Elementary, My Dear Gertie
Moms in Black, A Mom Squad Caper
Once Upon a Romance
Finding Mr. Right

Children's Chapter Book
The Magic Paintbrush

Nonfiction
Top Ten Reasons Your Novel is Rejected
House Unauthorized
Bake, Love, Write
We'd Rather Be Writing

Elementary, My Dear Gertie

LOIS WINSTON

Cover design by L. Winston

ISBN-13: 978-1-940795-24-9

DEDICATION

This novella is for all of my fans who asked for more Gertie.

ONE

First comes love, then comes marriage, then comes Nori pushing a baby carriage. As I stared at the words stitched on the needlepoint pillow, my cheeks burned. Leave it to my mother to transform Christmas morning into an Embarrass-Nori-Fest. Since arriving back in Ten Commandments, Iowa two days ago, I'd put up with non-stop innuendos, commentary, and sermons about my living-in-sin lifestyle and ticking biological clock. However, with the gift I'd just opened, Mom had gone too far. Way too far.

"Smile and say, 'thank you'," advised Gertie, my childhood imaginary friend who'd come back to haunt me nearly two years ago.

"Haunt you? Humph! If it weren't for me, you'd be pulling espresso shots at Starbucks or asking, 'Do you want fries with that?' Who's responsible for you becoming the hottest talk-radio personality in all of New York?"

I glanced across the room to where Mac, my boss and significant other, sat wedged between my father and an overabundance of handmade throw pillows, Mom's latest *craft du mois* on her cable TV show. Mac wore a patient expression on his face and a hand-knit red and green striped tie draped around his neck.

Ties were September's *craft du mois*. Thanks to Connie Stedworth, America's craft maven and my mother—not necessarily in that order—males all over America opened gifts of knit, crocheted, painted, appliquéd, cross stitched, hand-woven, or patchwork quilted ties this morning. Unless they were Jewish, in which case they'd received their handmade neckwear ten days ago on the first night of Hanukkah.

Gertie interrupted my necktie digression with a shrill question. *"Sure Mackenzie Randolph hired you, but who's responsible for you meeting him? If it weren't for yours truly, you'd have walked right past him and kept on walking."*

Highly unlikely, given the only available seat in Bean Around the Block that day was the empty one across the table from Mac, but Gertie's a credit hog.

"I take credit where credit's due. You'd have a hard time surviving without me, Honora Stedworth. Besides, who came crying to whom for help? I was doing just fine, thank-you-very-much, enjoying my hard earned and richly deserved retirement after dealing with your childhood and adolescence. Not an easy job by any stretch of the imagination, I might add."

So what type of 401K plans are available to imaginary friends?

"Save the snarkiness for your listeners. It's Christmas. Suck up your pride, and thank your mother. You've only got five days to go before you fly back to New York."

I stole a peek at the anniversary clock fighting for space among a multitude of Christmas cards covering the mantle. Five days, three hours, and forty-seven minutes if our flight departed on time, but who's counting?

"Earth to Nori. I don't suppose you've noticed that everyone is staring at you, waiting for you to hold up the gift and say something?"

Pushy, isn't she? I gritted my teeth, plastered a smile on my face, and said, "How sweet. Thank you, Mom." But I kept the pillow firmly planted in the cardboard box on my lap. No need to expand the Embarrass-Nori-Fest into an Embarrass-Nori-and-Mac-Fest. So far, Mom had behaved herself in front of Mac, reserving her innuendos, commentary, and sermons to times when he was out of earshot. I hoped to maintain the status quo.

"The pastel colors will work for either a boy or a girl," said Mom.

Not that there was even the hint of a boy or a girl bun in the oven. And none planned. I folded the red and green tissue paper back over the pillow and reached for the cardboard lid.

Mom jumped to her feet. "What are you doing, Nori? Hold it up. Show everyone."

By *everyone* Mom meant the two other people in the living room—my father and Mac—but I'm sure Dad had already seen Mom's less-than-subtle needlepoint missive. Her message was aimed directly at me and my partner-in-sin.

However, in Ten Commandments, Iowa we were more like partners-in-absentia. Or maybe that should be partners-in-*abstaintia*. Mac and I had been sharing both an apartment and a bed in New York for more than a year and a half, but this was our first trip as a couple to visit my parents. We'd avoided a Christmas trek to the Midwest last year by booking a trip to Europe. I'd been dealing with the fallout ever since.

So here we were. And although my parents were aware of our

living arrangement in New York, they chose to ignore it, refusing to set foot in our apartment whenever Mom's burgeoning empire brought them east.

Share a room with Mac under their roof? Never going to happen. Not until we'd exchanged *I do's* in front of my uncle, the Reverend Zechariah Stedworth. And my mother had no qualms about employing every available means of communication to hammer that fact into me—including needlepoint. Frankly, I was surprised not to see a billboard directed toward me as we pulled into town.

"For heaven's sake!" Mom strode through a floor of discarded wrapping paper and ribbons, grabbed the box off my lap, and headed toward Mac. "I spent hours stitching this for you. The least you can do is share it with your...your—." She frowned at Mac.

Dad cleared his throat. "Significant other, dear."

Mom glared at Dad, then shot a hostile nod in Mac's direction. Identical round, red spots surfaced on each of her cheeks. "If he's so significant, why aren't they married? Or at least engaged?" She dumped the box on Mac's lap and marched toward the kitchen.

So much for maintaining the status quo.

"Connie," called Dad, "come back."

Mom muttered under her breath, "If I don't get that bird in the oven...and then there's the cranberry relish...and the yams..."

Dad shook his head at both Mac and me before he hauled himself off the sofa and followed Mom into the kitchen.

I sighed.

Mac sighed.

Then he took a look at the needlepoint pillow and sighed again, this time more forcefully before he read the embroidered phrase aloud. *"First comes love, then comes marriage, then comes*

Nori pushing a baby carriage."

When God was passing out the Subtle genes, my mother was probably off *faux* finishing something.

A sheepish grin spread across Mac's face. "And you were worried I'd be bored in your little hometown?"

"Bored and embarrassed. So which is worse?"

He laughed. "I'm definitely not bored." Then he motioned toward the front door. "Think we can duck out of here for a while?"

Since Mom's crafting talents didn't extend to chastity belts (yet,) she wasn't satisfied with placing Mac and me in separate bedrooms at either end of the second floor. When we arrived, I was assigned my childhood bedroom, and Mac was relegated to a room at the Ten Commandments Inn, the only motel in town.

Mom couldn't control what went on in New York, but she was determined a mile would separate me from temptation as long as Mac and I were on her turf. And given that the establishment was owned and operated by Mom's second-cousin Maude-Ann Krissendorf, I suspected an additional pair of eyes had been pressed into service to deter any possible hanky-panky.

"I'd better go make nice first," I said.

"Good idea. Fill a thermos with coffee while you're in there."

"What for?"

"Knowing your mother, if we take the car, she'll come after us with a shotgun. We'd better hoof it."

I glanced out the window. Anyone who wished for a white Christmas had never lived in Iowa in December. An inch of fresh snow had accumulated since the plow had come down the street a few hours ago. More continued to fall, lightly but steadily. White windblown whorls danced in gusts down the empty street.

A perfect morning to curl up in bed, but the bed in question was a mile away, and Mac was right. Taking the car would set off Mom's internal radar. My embarrassment over the needlepoint pillow would pale in comparison to having her barge in on us after she'd cajoled Maude-Ann out of a passkey. Or maybe she already had one stashed away for just such an emergency.

I headed for the kitchen while Mac grabbed our coats and boots. "We're going for a walk," I said, coming up behind Mom and pecking her cheek.

She stiffened at my touch, her hands freezing in mid-stuff of the turkey. Then her shoulders sagged, and the stiffness drained from her spine. She withdrew her hands from inside old Tom, gave them a quick rinse at the sink, then grabbed a dish towel. Finally, her hands still damp, she turned to face me and offered a weak smile as she tucked a few strands of my always unmanageable riot of strawberry blonde curls behind my ear. "Nori, I only want what's best for you, dear."

"I know, Mom." I saw no purpose in pointing out that at twenty-eight years of age, I should be the one to determine what was best for me. We'd had this particular argument too many times. "We'll be back in plenty of time for me to help you with the side dishes."

"Isn't it too cold for a walk?" asked my father, pausing in his yam-peeling duties.

I glanced over at him as I filled the thermos from the coffee pot Mom always kept simmering with fresh brew. Did he suspect we'd tramp a mile through snow and slush for a quickie? Would he spill the beans?

I never knew how to read Dad lately. He'd always been the more conservative of the two, but several scandals involving members of his family, along with Mom's foray into the world of celebrity, had changed him. When Dad was forced to confront the fact that not everyone marches to the tune of his particular drummer, he abdicated his role as mayor and moral arbiter of Ten Commandments, not to mention the world.

Still, I knew it was difficult for him to accept that his only daughter was no longer as pure as that white stuff falling from the heavens.

I crossed over to the kitchen table and kissed the top of his balding head. "We'll bundle up." He eyed me as if he saw right through me but went back to yam peeling without saying another word.

"Wear your boots," said Mom. "And don't forget a scarf and gloves."

"Of course." Pushing twenty-nine by the calendar, still nine in my mother's eyes. Some things would never change.

I met Mac in the front hallway. He slipped the thermos into a backpack while I shrugged into my parka.

"Desperate, aren't we?" asked Gertie as Mac and I crunched our way down the road, being careful to dodge black ice and mounds of frozen slush.

Desperate didn't begin to describe the jumble of emotions inside me. I loved my parents, but I loved them a lot more when they were in Iowa, and I was in New York. After two days in Ten Commandments, I had a lot of pent-up frustration to burn off. I figured I had two choices: sex or matricide. I opted for the more pleasurable and less sinful of the two.

~*~

Twenty minutes later, after scoping out the grounds to make certain Maude-Ann was nowhere in sight, Mac and I skulked half-frozen into his motel room. "I hate snow," I said, yanking the scarf from around my neck and tossing it onto the dresser. "I hate Iowa!" I continued, removing my coat, and dumped it on top of the scarf. "And I really hate manipulative mothers!"

"PMSing, are we?" asked Gertie. *"Maybe you need some chocolate."*

I'm not PMSing, and I don't need chocolate. Mom's actions, not to mention her gift, were ample justification to unleash my inner Terrible Two self.

And speaking of that gift, I turned in time to see Mac removing the offensive needlepoint from his backpack. "Why did you bring that?" I grabbed the pillow and hurled it across the room, missing by less than a millimeter the peeling finish on the faux brass desk lamp with its scuffed faux leather shade. The pillow ricocheted off the wall and skittered under the bed.

"For her next trick, Nori will drop to the floor, pound her fists, and kick her feet, while simultaneously wailing at the top of her lungs."

I just might. "How could my mother humiliate me like this?"

"Could be worse," said Mac. "At least she didn't wait until later this afternoon when you'll have a house full of company."

He had a point. There were many degrees of humiliation. Keeping mine within the immediate family was benign compared to the same scene playing out in front of dozens of cousins, aunts, and uncles.

"So that's why you brought the pillow with you? To leave it here?"

His face lit up in one of his Dennis-the-Menace grins as he bent into a sweeping bow, and that one stubborn lock of chestnut hair that was notorious for not staying in place, fell across his right eye. "Your knight in shining armor to the rescue, m'lady."

I curtsied. "Thank you, m'lord. Definitely one of your finer Sir Walter Raleigh moments. I will be forever in your debt."

"I'm counting on it." Mac dropped to his knees and sprawled across the god-awful orange shag carpet. I'd never had cause to enter one of the Inn's rooms prior to this visit back to Ten Commandments. Apparently, Maude-Ann hadn't upgraded the motel's décor since she inherited the place from her parents back in the last century. With a grunt, Mac reached under the bed to retrieve the pillow. When he stood up, both the left arm of his sweater and the needlepoint were covered in gray dust bunnies.

Looked like sometime in the last century was also the last time anyone had bothered to run a vacuum under the bed. "So much for cleanliness being next to godliness," I said. "I guess Maude-Ann missed that sermon."

Mac swatted the dust off the pillow. "You've got to give her props, Nori."

"Maude-Ann? For what?"

"Not Maude-Ann. Your mother. For *chutzpah*." Mac isn't Jewish, but like most native New Yorkers, certain ethnic words and phrases are a common part of his vocabulary. I lived in Manhattan all of a week before I learned that *chutzpah* means *balls*, and I'm not talking about the pink rubber bouncy kind. Having lived his entire life within the five boroughs, Mac is practically fluent in Yiddish, Spanish, and Ebonics. After living in the city since graduating from college, I'm not that far behind him.

Mac held the pillow inches from his face and squinted in the dim light cast by the low-watt bulb of the only working lamp in the room, the same lamp I'd nearly killed with my off-target pitch. I'd been aiming for the trash can. In a sing-song voice he reread the message stitched within a border of pastel-colored hearts. *"First comes love, then comes marriage, then comes Nori pushing a baby carriage."*

I groaned. "Sorry about that." As much of a nightmare being back in Ten Commandments was for me, it had to be a gazillion times worse for Mac. "At least there's normally over a thousand miles separating us. Imagine if Mom had decided to establish her business in New York."

Nearly two years ago, my mother suffered a menopausal meltdown, left my father, and showed up, with suitcases and craft supplies in tow, at my Greenwich Village apartment door. Within hours, Connie Stedworth, the pickled beets and decoupage queen of Ten Commandments, Iowa, had charmed the ultra-sophisticated New York veneer off Hyman Perth, my upstairs neighbor. Quicker than a *glissando* bibbity-bobbity-boo, Perth, an entrepreneurial Svengali of sorts, transformed Mom into the next Martha Stewart.

In the course of a few hours, the assistance of the Bergdorf Goodman spa and personal shopper, and my purloined American Express card, the woman who used to sport an Eisenhower-era graying pageboy and wear dresses left over from the set of *Little House on the Prairie*, discovered John Barrett, Donna Karan, and Manolo Blahnik. Life hasn't been the same since.

The former country bumpkin now heads a multi-million-dollar enterprise that includes a line of home décor products, a monthly magazine, the aforementioned cable TV show, and her own army of groupies known as Connie's Crafters. Luckily for me, she reconciled with Dad and moved back to Ten Commandments to establish her empire.

As busy as Mom is, she hasn't given up on her quest for

grandchildren. My future progeny are her Holy Grail, and as far as she's concerned, I'd better get busy conceiving them because she's already behind Leona Shakelmeyer seven to zip. Leona has been Mom's arch enemy ever since high school, and she loves nothing more than flaunting her grandchildren in Mom's face. That means Mac and I have to marry. Yesterday wouldn't be too soon. Hence, the Christmas present from Hell.

"You can't throw it out," said Mac. "She's going to expect to see it the next time she comes to New York."

"How? She refuses to set foot in our apartment."

"That could change."

"Expect Hell to freeze over first." I rubbed my palms up and down my arms. Even the heat of my anger couldn't ward off the chill that permeated my body. I glanced around the room until I spied the thermostat. "Mind turning that a few degrees above sub-zero?"

"Can't."

"Why not?"

"I don't have the key."

"Maude-Ann locks the thermostat?" This I had to see for myself. I crossed the room. Sure enough, a locked mesh housing surrounded the thermostat which was set at fifty-eight degrees. "Unbelievable!"

Mac tossed the pillow onto the bed and opened his arms. "Come here. I'll warm you."

BOOM!

The next moment I was in his arms, but neither the frigid temperature nor my raging hormones had propelled me. And instead of being sprawled across a yucky gold paisley bedspread, we lay in a heap, covered in chunks of drywall, plaster dust, and what used to be a cheap pine dresser.

Mac shoved to his feet, pulling me with him. I heard the crackling sound of flames, felt the heat of fire, but the air was too thick with settling debris and dark, acrid smoke to see more than a strange orangey glow. We stumbled outside through a gaping hole where the front window had been just minutes before, broken glass crunching under our feet.

"Are you okay?" asked Mac once we'd put a parking lot's distance between ourselves and what was quickly becoming the former site of the Ten Commandments Inn.

Even with the fire department right down the road, the old clapboard structure would be nothing but smoldering ashes before the volunteers made their way to the station. Luckily, Mac was Maude-Ann's only occupant. Ten Commandments had never been a tourist mecca by any stretch of the imagination. Most people who came to town were relatives who stayed with family. The occasional outsider and those passing through on their way elsewhere usually opted for the Motel 6 ten miles down the road in Badger Bluffs. At the Ten Commandments Inn, the *No* was never lit on the vacancy sign.

I gulped in fresh air and coughed out a cloud of smoke. "I think so."

Flames, fanned by the wind whipping across the snow-covered fields surrounding the Inn, quickly consumed the structure. A moment later, the roof above the room we'd run from collapsed inward. Bright orange embers shot skyward like Fourth of July rockets. I shuddered, not just from the frigid temperatures but from the realization that we could have been killed.

"I'm no fire expert," said Mac, "but I don't think this was an accident." He pulled his phone from his pocket. "Can I just call

911?"

I took the phone from him and punched in the number for the fire house, but I could already hear sirens coming from down the street. Word travels fast in Ten Commandments; explosions travel even faster. This one had probably been heard clear across the county.

"Are you saying someone deliberately set the fire?"

"Unless it was a gas explosion, but I didn't smell any gas."

"Neither did I. But why would someone want to burn down the Ten Commandments Inn?"

Mac shrugged. "Maybe Maude-Ann is tired of taking care of the Bates Motel and wants the insurance money so she can retire to Florida."

I thought about that for a moment. Then I remembered something. "No. Dad's cousin Josiah has a construction company, and he's been after Maude-Ann to sell to him for years. Maude-Ann has some strange attachment to this place. Even if she weren't such a tightwad, I don't think she'd change anything from when her parents owned the Inn. It would be like erasing their existence or desecrating their memory."

"Nori, it's a motel, not a shrine."

"Not to Maude-Ann. This is...was the only thing she had left of her parents. According to my mother, Maude-Ann was a late-in-life, only child. Her parents doted on her, but she was barely out of her teens when they died. She never married. This motel is her life." Not that it was much of a life. How could Maude-Ann make a profit on a motel that stood ninety percent empty most of the year?

A moment later the first of the fire trucks pulled into the parking lot. The idea of arson seemed absurd to me. There had to be a logical explanation for the explosion and subsequent fire. Besides, I had a more personal problem about to transpire. I groaned at the realization. "This place is about to be overrun with townspeople, most of whom are my relatives."

"Tongues will be a-wagging," said Gertie.

Tell me something I don't know.

"Want to make a run for it?" asked Mac.

"A tempting idea. Think anyone would believe we were just out for a Christmas morning stroll?"

"Soot covered and coatless? Even the good citizens of Ten Commandments aren't that naïve, but that's the least of our problems," he said.

"The least?"

"Absolutely. How are you going to explain the missing needlepoint pillow to your mother?"

"This should be good," said Gertie.

Only if you're a Torquemada groupie. The pillow was toast. I groaned again, this time loud enough to be heard all the way to Badger Bluffs.

~*~

The best part of growing up in a small town is that everyone knows everyone else. This comes in handy during times of crisis and disasters. The worst part of growing up in a small town is that everyone knows everyone else's business, whether you want them to or not. Within minutes the parking lot was jammed with half the residents of Ten Commandments. Some came to help; others came to gawk.

A swarm of town busybodies encircled Mac and me. Someone tossed warm but itchy woolen blankets across our shoulders, even though the heat from the fire kept us plenty warm. Someone else thrust steaming cups of coffee into our hands.

Then the inquisition began—rapid-fire questions, most having little to do with the fire and everything to do with innate nosiness. The Prodigal Daughter of Ten Commandments had returned to the fold, a man by her side, and the two of them were standing coatless outside a burning motel.

"What are you doing at the Inn, Nori?"

"Who's this man with you, Nori?"

"Did you start the fire, Nori? Did he?"

"What happened to your coats?"

I huddled next to Mac, sipped the coffee, and ignored all the questions flying at me. You'd think the ballsy biddies of Ten Commandments would have better things to do Christmas morning than play paparazzi.

"Apparently not," said Gertie. *"And if you don't speak to them, they'll just let their imaginations go to work."*

Do I care? Let the rumors fly.

I stood on tiptoe and craned my neck to scan the ever-growing crowd. "If Mom and Dad aren't here yet," I whispered to Mac, "they will be soon. Someone is bound to call them. Life will be a lot simpler if we slip into the house while they're on their way here."

"Until we have to explain what happened to our coats," said Mac. "And the needlepoint pillow."

"One crisis at a time, please."

I was about to suggest we inch our way to the back of the crowd, then cut a mad dash through Ralph Shakelmeyer's field (even though the snow was probably knee high and we risked frostbite,) when one of the firemen yelled, "There's a body in here!"

TWO

A collective gasp sprang from the mouths of my inquisitors. They eyed Mac as if they were memorizing his every feature in case they had to pick him out of a lineup at some later date. We don't get many strangers in Ten Commandments, so it stood to reason whatever had happened, he was the most likely suspect, even though Ten Commandments, contrary to its name, was a veritable Peyton Place of scandal, much of which involved my god-fearing relatives.

The next thing I knew Uncle Jonah Stedworth had pushed his way through the biddy throng and ushered Mac and me inside his police chief's cruiser.

"We didn't do anything," I told him.

He eyed us skeptically, focusing on the blankets wrapped around our bodies. "Right," he muttered, but he didn't make eye contact, and he didn't dare pass judgment. How could he, given his own recent fall from grace? Nearly two years ago Dad had walked in on Uncle Jonah diddling Aunt Florrie. FYI, Aunt Florrie is married to Dad's other brother, the Reverend Zechariah Stedworth. And that's only one of the many scandals to hit Ten Commandments in the years since I left home.

"Stay here," said Uncle Jonah.

Once we were settled into the back seat, he jacked up the heat before leaving. "Maybe he just wanted to get us away from the gossipmongers," said Mac.

"If you believe that, there's this bridge in Brooklyn..."

I ignored Gertie, my attention riveted on the body bag being carried out of what was left of the room next to the one Mac had occupied. "I thought Maude-Ann said you were her only guest."

"She did," said Mac.

"Then who's in the body bag?"

~*~

As it turned out, Uncle Jonah was less interested in gossips and more interested in taking statements from Mac and me. Once it became clear there were no other victims and no possibility of saving the Inn, he put a deputy in charge of the scene and drove us to the police station. On the way we passed Dad's dark green Chevy Tahoe heading toward the Inn.

"I don't even want to think about the earful they're going to get from the gossip brigade," I whispered to Mac.

Instead of an interrogation room, we were ushered into Uncle Jonah's office. "Sit," he said, indicating two battered wooden chairs across from his equally battered desk. He closed his office door, shrugged out of his parka and tossed it and his hat onto pegs attached to the back of the door. As he lowered himself into his chair, he expelled a deep sigh of weariness that shuddered through his entire body. "Okay, Nori. What the hell happened back there?"

"How should I know? One minute Mac and I are standing in his room talking; the next minute the Inn is exploding around us."

"You didn't see or hear anything unusual?"

"Nothing."

Uncle Jonah turned to Mac. "What about you, son?"

Mac shook his head. "Like Nori said, nothing. No sounds of other people. No smell of gas or smoke that might have warned us something was wrong. Everything was quite normal until it wasn't. After the explosion, the room immediately filled with this dense, gritty black smoke. We managed to escape only because the window blew out. I grabbed Nori and headed in the direction of the cold air."

"Maude-Ann said Mac was the only guest," I added. "Who died?"

"I won't know that until Phineas takes a closer look at the body," said Uncle Jonah. "It sure as heck wasn't a pretty sight. Totally beyond recognition. I've got one of my deputies trying to track down Maude-Ann to see who was staying in that room. Could be the person checked in late last night or early this morning."

Phineas was Phineas Draymore, the county coroner. He was also the owner of the Draymore Funeral Home and the husband of Mom's best friend Marjorie. How he was supposed to identify a stranger was beyond me. The county coroner was an elected position. Phineas's expertise was more in formaldehyde than forensics.

"There were no cars in the parking lot," I said. "And we didn't hear anyone next door." Given the motel's cheap construction, chances were good Mac would have heard something last night, even if it was only a toilet flushing or the squeak of bedsprings.

"Doesn't mean no one was there," said Uncle Jonah. "Could be a couple and one of them left to run an errand before you showed up. The other one might've still been asleep."

His speculation made no sense to me. "What kind of errand would a stranger be running on Christmas morning in Ten Commandments? It's not like anything is open around here today."

"There could be any number of possibilities," said Uncle Jonah. "How 'bout you leave the police work to the pros, Nori?"

I half expected the old chauvinist to walk over and pat me on the head the way he used to when I was a kid.

"Welcome back to Ten Commandments," said Gertie. *"To him, you are still a kid."*

Too true. When I'm pushing fifty, my relatives will still be calling me Little Nori Stedworth.

I bit back the caustic retort perched on the tip of my tongue. After all, it was Christmas. "Of course, Uncle Jonah, but since you have the aftermath of this fire and the death of an unidentified stranger on your hands—"

"Murder," said Phineas Draymore as he rushed into the room. He tossed a Ziploc bag on top of the papers scattered across Uncle Jonah's desk. Mac, Uncle Jonah, and I leaned over and stared at the single blood-stained bullet inside the sandwich bag. "Someone shot Maude-Ann Krissendorf right through the heart. I'm guessing the killer probably started the fire to cover up the murder."

THREE

"Maude-Ann? Murdered?" Uncle Jonah picked up the evidence bag and stared at the bullet. "I suppose you don't need much skill as a coroner when you find a bullet lodged in someone's chest, Phineas. But how the hell do you know it's Maude-Ann? The body was pretty much toast."

Phineas cleared his throat and nodded toward where Mac and I still sat. "Show a little respect for the deceased, Jonah. Nori here was related to Maude-Ann."

Uncle Jonah pulled his attention from the bullet and looked at Mac and me as if he'd forgotten we were sitting right across from him. He indicated the open door with a wave of his pudgy hand. "You two can go."

I wasn't going anywhere. If there was a killer loose in Ten Commandments, I wanted as much information as possible, and that included how Phineas Draymore knew the dead woman was Maude-Ann. "How can you be sure it's Maude-Ann," I asked him.

Phineas ignored me, instead directing his answer to Uncle

Jonah. "You know any other woman in these parts who's got an extra pinkie finger on her left hand?"

"Well, no," said Uncle Jonah, "but that's hardly conclusive evidence."

"I've got conclusive evidence, Jonah. As soon as I noticed the extra finger, I called Doc Petterschmidt and had him walk over Maude-Ann's dental records. They're a match. Right down to her last filling. And one other thing," continued Phineas. "Based on the postmortem lividity of the corpse, Maude-Ann wasn't killed where your boys found her. She was moved at some point after she was shot."

Hmm . . . apparently Phineas knew something about forensics, after all.

"Any idea when she was killed?" asked Uncle Jonah.

"Hard to tell," said Phineas, "given that lividity can set in anywhere from around twenty minutes or so to a few hours, and we've got the fire messing with the postmortem."

"Why would anyone want to kill Maude-Ann?" I asked.

Phineas shot a sideways glance at Uncle Jonah. Uncle Jonah screwed up his mouth and shook his head. "This here's an official murder investigation now. All information's on a need-to-know basis." He pointed at the open office door. "And you two don't qualify as needing to know."

"So I guess this means we're dismissed?" That came out a bit snarkier than I intended, but I really didn't care. Something was up with Uncle Jonah and Phineas. They knew something. Something that had to do with Maude-Ann. And maybe her murder.

"For now. But don't leave town."

"Excuse me?"

"You heard me, Honora. Right now, you two are the only leads I have. Consider yourselves material witnesses until you hear otherwise."

"We didn't witness anything!"

"Don't make me get a court order," said Uncle Jonah. "And tell your mother I'm probably going to be late for dinner."

I didn't bother acknowledging him. Mac and I gathered our scratchy blankets around our shoulders and stood to leave. However, before we made it to the doorway, Mom rushed in, Dad close enough behind her that when she stopped short to keep from barreling into me, he barreled into her.

"Tell her yourself," I said over my shoulder.

"Tell me what?" Mom first scrutinized me in all my coatless, disheveled, smoke and soot-covered glory, then turned her wrath on Uncle Jonah. "Jonah Stedworth, you're not arresting your niece, are you?" Then without taking a breath or waiting for an answer, she turned her attention to Mac and me. "And just what were the two of you doing in that motel room?"

"Not what you're insinuating," I said. "And by the way, Mom, we're fine, thanks to Mac who saved our lives."

That was when my mother lost it. Right there in Uncle Jonah's office, the adrenaline that must have propelled her from the moment she learned we were in the motel at the time of the fire, gave way to the fear it had masked. A torrent of diluvian proportion sprang from her eyes as she grabbed me in her arms and blubbered huge sobs of relief. I'm sure she never would have forgiven herself, had something happened to me, thanks to her antiquated attitudes. Lucky for both of us, we'd never find out.

~*~

An hour later, we were back at the house, cleaned up, and helping Mom get ready for the company she expected. Poor Mac had lost all his clothes in the fire, except those he'd been wearing, and was forced to borrow clothes from Dad. At least he and Dad were only a few inches apart in height, so the borrowed pants weren't too short. But weight-wise? Let's just say Mac would have plenty of room for expansion when we sat down for Christmas dinner.

Fashion-wise? I didn't care how dorky Mac looked in Dad's less-than-designer duds. Dorky and alive trumped cool-looking and dead any day.

However, I was still steaming over Uncle Jonah's demand that Mac and I remain in Ten Commandments until he said otherwise. "He could keep us here until he solves this murder," I whispered as Mac helped me place the leaves in Mom's dining room table.

She and Dad were in the kitchen, and I didn't want them knowing that Uncle Jonah had threatened us with a court order. Knowing Mom, she'd offer to run down to the county courthouse for him if it meant keeping me from going back to New York. "He's just the sort to do it, too. I don't think he's forgiven Dad for walking in on him and Aunt Florrie. And he probably blames Dad for blabbing all over town about it, but my father would never do anything of the sort."

"So because your uncle cheated on his wife and your father caught him at it, we have to suffer? That kind of reasoning defies logic."

I set the final leaf in place. "I know," I said with a whoosh as I pushed the table from one end and he pushed from the other. "But what can we do? Solve the murder ourselves?"

Mac placed and locked the table pads while I hunted through the sideboard for Mom's Christmas linens. "If we're stuck here for the duration," he said, "we may as well do whatever we can to speed things up. How confident are you that your uncle can handle a murder investigation?"

"Let's put it this way," I said, pulling out the poinsettia decorated damask I'd been searching for, "I don't think my uncle is capable of investigating anything more than a lost dog, but he's got way too much pride to ask for help."

Mac grabbed one end of the tablecloth and together we settled it evenly onto the table. "That's what I was afraid of. So which one of us is Watson and which one is Holmes?"

"I did play the violin for a few years."

"Really? And here I thought I knew everything there was to know about you."

"Hey, a girl has to have some secrets to keep the romance fresh."

"So, were you in the high school orchestra?"

"Elementary school, my dear Watson."

~*~

Since my relatives had never learned the fine art of minding their own business, I had prepped Mac ahead of time for a typical Ten Commandments Christmas Inquisition. "Expect a nonstop barrage of questions from my aunts and female cousins."

"About?"

"What do you think? About why we're not married yet and what are we waiting for?"

Mac lowered his head and kissed the tip of my nose. "Hey, you think I can't handle a few gossipy middle-aged Iowa housewives and their equally gossipy daughters?"

"All as rabid as my mother? These women live for weddings and babies, neither of which I've produced so far. I'm giving the sisterhood a bad name."

Today was no typical Christmas, though. Maude Ann's murder had knocked the return of the Prodigal Daughter out of contention as Topic Number One on the gossip hit parade.

"Leave it to Maude-Ann to get herself murdered on Christmas," said my less-than-charitable Aunt Florrie. She scowled at the empty chair and place setting Mom had insisted upon in honor of a woman who would never again enjoy a Christmas dinner with us. Or anyone else, for that matter. "She always was an odd bird."

"People who live in glass parsonages..." I muttered from behind my napkin, loud enough that my mother shot me one of her looks. I shot one right back at her. Adulterous reverend's wives have no business bad-mouthing anyone, least of all poor dead Maude-Ann, even if she was one the tightest tightwads in all of Iowa. I still couldn't get over how she kept the room thermostats locked.

"First murder ever in Ten Commandments," said Uncle Zechariah. "This town is going to heck in a hand basket." He directed that last comment across the table at Uncle Jonah. I guess the good Reverend hadn't yet found total forgiveness in his heart with regard to his wife and brother.

"I don't care how odd she was," Mom said. "Maude-Ann certainly didn't deserve to die the way she did. And whoever killed her nearly killed Nori."

"And Mac," I added.

"Just what were the two of you doing over there this morning?" asked Aunt Florrie.

I offered her a saccharine smile. "Nothing you haven't done."

"Nori!" Mom's face flushed the color of her prize-winning pickled beets. "The children!"

She referred to my cousins' kids, a half dozen pre-pubescent rugrats sitting at a separate table in the living room and totally oblivious to the nearby adults. "Not paying any attention to us, Mom."

No one knows how everyone found out about Aunt Florrie and Uncle Jonah. Dad swears he told no one, and I believe him. Dad's not the gossipmonger type, and I don't believe he's ever told a lie in his entire life. Besides, he would have been too embarrassed by the X-rated scene he stumbled upon that day. Just one more Ten Commandments mystery that may never be solved. But Maude-Ann's murder had pushed Ten Commandment's most recent scandal from everyone's mind.

"Until you just reminded them," said Gertie.

Florrie deserved it. And to think she used to be one of my favorite relatives. Every Christmas we'd bake gingerbread boys and girls together, and she'd let me decorate them with way too many M&M's. Now I can't even look at a gingerbread man, let alone an M&M, without conjuring up an image of her and Uncle Jonah, their naked, flabby, fat butts ...well, you get the picture.

"Ewww!"

You've got that right, I told Gertie. No matter how liberated and liberal-minded I am, there are some things that definitely fall into the TMI category. At the top of the list is any of my relatives having sex, especially adulterous sex. Still, the image had branded itself in my brain, and I'd only heard about it. Can you imagine my poor father?

The man in question turned the topic of conversation back to Maude-Ann's murder. "Any suspects?" he asked his brother.

"You know I can't comment on an ongoing investigation," said Uncle Jonah.

"You're investigating?" Aunt Pauline turned to her husband and in a voice that left no question she, too, hadn't yet forgiven him for cheating on her, said, "The closest you've ever come to investigating a murder was that time LeRoy drove his pickup through the Shakelmeyer's pig pen and killed Ralph's Blue-Ribbon hog."

"I did graduate from the police academy," said Uncle Jonah.

"Thirty years ago," countered Aunt Pauline. "You should call in the Department of Criminal Investigations before you botch this up, too."

"Definitely hasn't forgiven him," said Gertie.

Not that there was any doubt. If Aunt Pauline and Uncle Jonah were seated any farther from each other, they'd be in separate counties. Rumor had it, Uncle Jonah now slept in the storm cellar. Rumor also had it that Aunt Florrie wasn't Uncle Jonah's first and only dalliance, nor was he hers. Did I mention Ten Commandments didn't exactly live up to its holy name?

"Your cousin Josiah's the only one with a motive," my cousin Gideon said to Dad. "Everyone knows he's been after Maude-Ann to buy her out for years."

"That makes no sense," said Mac, who had remained silent up to this point. "How would he benefit from her death?"

All my relatives turned to stare at him. "What do you mean?" asked Gideon.

"Unless Maude-Ann left the motel to Josiah in her will, how would killing her get him the property?"

"Why would Maude-Ann leave so much as a nickel to Josiah?" said Aunt Pauline. "They weren't even related."

"Exactly the point," said Mac.

"Maybe he thought he'd have better luck with whomever

inherits the place," said Gideon's wife Jeanie.

"Who's that?" asked Uncle Zechariah.

Mom cleared her throat. "I'm Maude-Ann's only living relative."

"And where were you this morning?" asked Aunt Florrie.

Mom jumped up so quickly, her chair pitched backwards and rammed into the sideboard. "You of all people, Florrie Stedworth, should think before hurling accusations."

I'd never seen my mother so angry. I'm not sure Dad had, either. He righted her chair and placed his hand on her arm to ease her back into her seat. "Connie—"

"Don't Connie me, Earnest! Who does that holier-than-thou whore think she is insulting me in my own home?" And then my mother did something so un-Connie-like that generations from now people living in Ten Commandments will still be talking about it. She grabbed Aunt Florrie's plate off the table and pointed to the front door. "Leave. Immediately. You are no longer welcome in my home, Florrie Stedworth."

A collective gasp rose from around the dining room table, followed by total silence. Even the kids stopped chattering and turned to see what was going on at the grown-up table where the grown-ups were acting far from grown-up.

I stole a glance at Mac and saw that he was fighting to keep from laughing his head off. "Anything but boring," he mouthed.

"Welcome to Ten Commandments," I said.

FOUR

Mom was still seething an hour after all the other guests had gone home, and she was taking her temper out on various inanimate objects as Dad, Mac, and I helped her clean up. I did notice, though, that she reined in her anger while washing her grandmother's china and crystal, only grumbling and muttering under her breath. She saved her outbursts for the unbreakable cookware that littered the kitchen table and counters.

"How dare she insinuate that I had something to do with Maude-Ann's death?" Mom asked no one in particular. "I was the only person in this town who cared about that poor woman! Didn't I give her a job? She was the first person I hired to help with the show. I made her my assistant because I knew she was barely getting by with what she made from that flea trap. And what would be my motive?"

"Which brings us back to Dad's cousin Josiah," I said. "You'd be happy to sell the place to him, wouldn't you?"

Mom thought for a moment, then shrugged. "I suppose. It's

not like I have any desire to run a motel."

"Josiah may have a perfectly legitimate alibi," said Dad. "Jonah doesn't even know when Maude-Ann died, and if he doesn't call in the state, like he's supposed to, he may never know. As soon as this case went from a fire investigation to a murder, he should have placed a call to the Department of Criminal Investigations. Besides, I wouldn't put too much stock in Phineas Draymore's ability to pinpoint time of death." He turned to Mac. "When was the last time you saw Maude-Ann?"

"I didn't. Not after I checked in."

"Which means Maude-Ann could have been killed up to two days ago," I said.

"We would have noticed the stench of rotting corpse," said Mac.

"Would we? Maude-Ann kept the thermostat in your room locked at fifty-eight degrees. She probably kept the heat off entirely in unoccupied rooms."

"The pipes would freeze," said Dad.

"If she kept the thermostat around thirty-five degrees, the pipes wouldn't freeze, and the body would stay refrigerated," said Mom, "slowing decomposition."

We all stared at her. "When did you become a forensics expert?" I asked.

She shrugged. "*Law & Order* reruns. I used to watch them when your father was mayor and never home in the evenings."

Ouch! I hope this conversation wasn't veering into *that* territory. Murder was a much safer topic.

"I thought that's when you worked on your crafts projects," Dad said.

"Ever hear of multitasking, Earnest?"

Once upon a time my mother was the quintessential *Nick at Night* housewife—June Cleaver, Harriet Nelson, and Donna Reed all wrapped up into one Connie Stedworth. Over the past couple of years Mom hit menopause, discovered her inner entrepreneur, and become the poster child for women's lib. But because she entered the movement forty years too late, she's making up for it with a vengeance, breathing down Martha Stewart's neck as her ratings soar and her ever-increasing product line outsells Martha's. Needless to say, life in the Stedworth domicile has been very different ever since Mom's first trip to New York.

"There is no way Joe would kill anyone," said Dad, moving the subject back to the original topic. "Besides, given the economic slowdown and how construction is at a standstill, I doubt he's even still interested in Maude-Ann's property."

"True," said Mom. "Maude-Ann hadn't mentioned him in months, and she used to complain to me every time he tried to buy her out."

"Who else would want her dead?" I asked.

"Beats me," said Mom. "Maude-Ann pretty much kept to herself."

"What about a disgruntled employee?" asked Mac.

Mom shook her head. "No staff. She had such little business that she cleaned the rooms herself."

That explained the decades of dust bunnies under the bed.

"Maybe the killer is someone who stayed at the inn and got pissed because he couldn't turn up the thermostat," I said. "Or maybe he gave Maude-Ann a bogus credit card, and when she confronted him, he shot her."

"If the killer was someone just passing through, we'll probably never learn the truth," said Dad.

But something about that look exchanged between Uncle Jonah and Phineas Draymore had me thinking Maude-Ann's murderer was no stranger to Ten Commandments. Besides, the sooner Mac and I figured out who the killer was, the sooner we'd be on a plane headed back to the safety and sanity of Manhattan.

"Let the sleuthing begin," said Gertie.

~*~

The next day Mac and I bundled up and headed back to the scene of the crime. Little was left of the Ten Commandments Inn. However, since the explosion and subsequent fire occurred in a room at the far end of the long, one-story structure, the fire fighters had managed to douse the flames before they totally consumed the opposite end of the building. The lobby and Maude-Ann's living quarters, situated directly behind the lobby, remained relatively unscathed except for being slightly singed, waterlogged, and sooty, not to mention partially blanketed with several inches of snow blown in through the broken windows.

"I'm willing to bet no one searched Maude-Ann's apartment," I said. "Maybe we'll find some clues inside."

Mac grabbed my arm as I started to step through the glassless plate glass window. "This is a crime scene. If we're caught, your uncle could toss us in jail."

"So we don't get caught. Besides, the crime scene is over there." I waved my mittened hand toward the other end of the parking lot. "This area isn't cordoned off."

Either Uncle Jonah had A) run out of yellow crime scene tape, B) gotten lazy and didn't bother to wrap the entire structure, or C) the tape around the lobby and apartment had fallen victim to last night's blizzard-strength winds and was now whipping around somewhere over Indiana. Knowing my uncle, my money was on B.

I bolstered my argument by adding, "We're only breaking the law if we cross over crime scene tape. No tape, no lawbreaking."

Mac gave me one of those I-wasn't-born-yesterday looks. "I didn't know you had a degree in criminal law."

I countered with a not-so-innocent grin. "Mom isn't the only Stedworth who watches *Law & Order* reruns." Or at least I did in my pre-Mac days. Now I'm usually engaged in another form of entertainment most evenings.

We made our way around the lobby counter to an open doorway that led into Maude-Ann's living quarters. "What a mess!" I said as I scanned a room that had evidently served as a combination living room, dining room, and kitchen. "The wind didn't do this." The place had been ransacked—drawers upended, cabinets and shelves emptied, cushions slashed, breakables smashed.

"Someone was definitely looking for something," said Mac.

"You think?" asked Gertie.

I ignored her snark and concentrated on the mess. "This makes no sense. What could Maude-Ann possibly have that someone would kill for? According to my mother, she lived only inches above the poverty line."

"Maybe the killer didn't know that," said Mac. "Or maybe what Maude-Ann had wasn't worth anything except to the killer."

I thought about that for a moment, not sure where Mac was going with it. Then it hit me. "You mean like something she was using to blackmail someone?"

He shrugged. "Possibly."

"I hardly think Maude-Ann was the blackmailing type. Then again, there was that odd exchange I caught between my uncle and

Phineas. What was up with that?"

"Who knows?" said Mac. "Blackmail does seem a bit odd, though, from what you've told me about Maude-Ann. More likely, she owned something that she didn't realize was valuable."

"That makes more sense. But what?"

"The family jewels?"

I shook my head as I sidestepped a toppled china hutch on my way to the bedroom. "I don't think there were any, but we should ask my mother. She'd know." Then I thought of something else, and it sent a shiver up my spine. "Whatever the killer was looking for, we have no idea whether or not he found it."

"And if not, he's probably still lurking around Ten Commandments," added Mac.

If that were the case, he'd be easy to spot. Strangers stick out in Ten Commandments like a Size Zero at a Weight Watchers meeting. The more troubling scenario was that the killer wasn't a stranger but a member of the community. Someone everyone knew and trusted. And if that were the case, it was imperative that we find him before we returned to New York. I wasn't about to leave my parents to the mercy of some local gone bad.

I stood in the middle of Maude-Ann's bedroom, surveying another mess. The killer had ransacked this room as thoroughly as the living room, leaving no nook or cranny unsearched, no bric-a-brac unsmashed. He'd even rifled through a box of tissues, scattering the now soggy wads of tissue across the floor. "Our first clue," I said, pointing to the empty box. "Whatever he was looking for, it's small enough to fit inside a tissue box."

"Unless he was just pissed at not finding what he was looking for and decided to trash the place for spite," said Mac.

"So much for my ah-ha moment." I sighed in frustration.

"What would Nancy Drew do?"

"Beats me," said Mac. "No adolescent boy would ever be caught dead reading Nancy Drew."

I decided to ignore his sexist comment. I learned a long time ago you have to cut guys some slack, given their Y chromosome handicap. You can't blame someone for a defect they're born with. "Fine. What would Encyclopedia Brown do?"

Mac shrugged. "Sorry. Never read any."

"Hardy Boys?"

"Nope."

"What did you read as a kid?"

Mac thought for a minute. "Mostly books about King Arthur and the Knights of the Round Table. And Tolkien. I devoured Tolkien."

"So what would Frodo do?"

"Kick your asses the hell out of here and right into lockup."

Mac and I spun around to find Uncle Jonah standing in the doorway, the nastiest of scowls planted across his face.

FIVE

"You're in deep caca now," said Gertie, always the master of understatement.

"What the hell are you two doing messing around my crime scene?"

"Looking for clues to Maude-Ann's murder," I said.

"And I told you to keep your nose out of this investigation, Honora. What's gotten into you? You used to listen to and respect your elders."

"That was back when I believed they were worthy of respect."

"Ouch!" Gertie winced. So did Mac. Okay, maybe that was going a tad too far. Honesty isn't always the best policy, especially when that honesty is directed toward a man with a gun. Even if he is your uncle.

"Your father had no business blabbing about that. All he did was cause everyone a lot of hurt and trouble."

"You know Dad better than that, Uncle Jonah. He didn't spill the beans about you and Aunt Florrie. Besides, you've got no right deflecting blame for your actions onto him or anyone else."

Uncle Jonah threw his hands up in the air, sank down on Maude-Ann's slashed mattress, and released a huge sigh. "You get to be my age, Nori, and haven't made a few mistakes, then you can throw stones."

"I'd rather spend time figuring out who killed Maude-Ann. You said we can't leave town until you find the killer. We can't hang around here waiting for you to figure things out, Uncle Jonah. We have jobs back in New York. And no offense, but when was the last time you investigated anything more serious than some stolen hubcaps or graffiti sprayed on the cannon in the town square?"

Uncle Jonah sprang to his feet, his already ruddy cheeks reddening several shades toward purple at the aspersion cast upon his record. "I'm a trained officer of the law, young lady. You want me to call in the state? They'll come down a whole lot harder on you, especially when they learn you've been tampering with evidence."

"We didn't touch anything!"

"Just being here compromises the investigation. Anyone finds out you were snooping, the case gets tossed out of court by some sleazebag defense lawyer."

I hadn't thought of that. I should have. Like I told Mac, Mom isn't the only Stedworth who watched *Law & Order* reruns. I mumbled an apology.

"Now go home," he said, then turned to Mac. "Son, you'll be doing all of us a huge favor if you make her stay put."

"How dare—"

Mac grabbed my arm. "Don't," he warned. He nodded to Uncle Jonah. "You don't have to worry, sir."

~*~

"How could you?" I demanded after Mac and I were back in the parking lot. "That philandering chauvinist pig had no right—"

Mac pulled me into his arms and shut me up with a kiss. "No fair," I groused after he pulled away.

"Choose your battles, Nori. You were pushing his buttons. If you kept it up, I really think he might have tossed you into the slammer just to show you who wields the real power around here."

I huffed out an icy cloud of exasperation. "You're right, of course. He just made me so mad."

"And he was right about one thing."

"What's that?"

"We don't want to be the reason a murder conviction gets tossed."

I kicked at a chunk of frozen snow. "I know, but this is so frustrating. We could be stuck here for weeks. Months, even! We'll lose our jobs! Our apartment!"

"Believe me, I'm not happy about that, either. We still have four days before our flight. Maybe something will turn up. For now, let's find out more about Maude-Ann from your mother."

~*~

When Mac and I returned to my parents' house, the four of us gathered around the kitchen table. Mom was torn up with guilt over Maude-Ann's death. She'd always thought of Maude-Ann as a slightly backward little sister who needed protection. Especially after Maude-Ann lost her parents years ago. For that reason, she was more than happy to discuss her deceased cousin with us.

"At least I won't feel like I failed her if I can help find her killer," she said. "Maybe if we all brainstorm, we'll come up with some answers. Lord knows, that sorry excuse for a sheriff won't make much progress toward solving the case."

Dad didn't seem at all upset about the disparaging remark directed toward his brother. Once upon a time, not too long ago, he would have defended Uncle Jonah from now until the Guernseys and Herefords came home. That was back when he admired and respected his brother. Before he'd caught him with his pants down—literally. Or maybe they were completely off. The particulars of that event definitely fell into the TMI category for me. I wasn't asking, and I didn't want anyone telling. As for now, I swear I heard him mutter something under his breath about how you could choose your friends, but you couldn't choose your blood relatives.

"Why don't we start by making a list of everyone who had dealings with Maude-Ann," offered Mac. "Then we go down the list, eliminating the people with an alibi for the two days prior to Christmas morning. Those without alibis, we speculate on possible motives."

It was as good a plan as any. I grabbed a pencil and pad from Mom's catch-all drawer, settled back into my chair, and drew a vertical line down the center of the top page. One column I labeled SUSPECTS and the other, MOTIVE. Josiah Stedworth came in as Suspect Number One, his motive, that he coveted Maude-Ann's property.

"Forget it," said Dad. "I called Joe last night after everyone went home. He and Ellie took the kids to Florida to spend Christmas with her parents. They left the day before you and Mac arrived. Not that I ever suspected him, mind you, but Maude-Ann was still alive the day after Joe left the state."

I ran a line through Suspect Number One. "Who else?" The room grew silent. I tapped the pencil eraser on the pad as the kitchen clock ticked away the seconds.

"The poor woman was shot through the heart," said Mac finally. "Someone must have had a beef with her."

Mom shook her head. "Maude-Ann was practically invisible. She pretty much kept to herself when she wasn't helping me."

"What about someone connected with your show?" I asked. "Was anyone ticked off at her for some reason?"

Mom leaned back in her chair and gazed upward. Her features tightened in thought, as if she hoped to find answers hidden within the various spider vein cracks that peppered the plaster ceiling. After another long moment passed, she said, "I can't imagine anything that would escalate to murder, either at the show or anywhere else. I'm stymied."

"What was her daily routine like?" asked Mac.

"Maude-Ann spent a few hours a day doing paperwork and making calls for me, usually never leaving my office. She attended church on Sundays but never got involved in any committees, and she didn't sing in the choir. Other than those things and doing her weekly marketing and errands, as far as I know, she rarely left the motel grounds."

"She was pretty much a loner for as long as I knew her," added Dad. "Not to speak ill of the dead, but she was the kind of woman who easily faded into the background. She reminded me of a skittish little mouse. Looked like one, too. Mousy hair. Mousy features. Your mother was the only person who paid any attention to her."

"If no one wanted Maude-Ann dead for any reason," said Mac. "Maybe it was just a burglary gone bad. Someone passing through and long gone by now."

"Except no one just passes through Ten Commandments," I

said. "It's not like the town is on a major highway."

"True," said Dad. "The only people who come to Ten Commandments are people who want to be here for some reason."

"And sometimes even they can't find us," added Mom. "I can't begin to tell you how many times people connected with my show have wound up lost trying to get here. You can barely find us on a map."

"So much for the brainstorming session," said Gertie.

"This is so frustrating!" I smacked the pencil down onto the pad. "How do you solve a murder when you have no suspects or motives?"

"There has to be a motive," said Mac. "Someone was definitely looking for something in her apartment. The place was ransacked."

"I can't imagine what he hoped to find," said Mom. "Maude-Ann had nothing of value other than the motel and the land it sat on. Maybe the burglar trashed the place out of frustration at not finding anything worth stealing."

"Why bother when he planned to set the place on fire to cover up the murder?" asked Mac.

"Unless the fire was an afterthought," I said. "Maybe he tore the place apart, hoping to find something. Then Maude-Ann walks in on him, and he shoots her. He drags her to one of the rooms, then torches the place to cover up the murder."

"Why not just set the fire where he killed her?" asked Mac. "Why drag the body all the way down to the other end of the motel when he risked being seen by someone?"

"Nothing about this murder makes any sense," said Mom. "Why should that? Maybe the killer was on drugs and was too hopped up for logic."

"Anyone in Ten Commandments cooking meth lately?" I asked Dad. "What's Cousin LeRoy up to these days?" Cousin LeRoy used to be the only black sheep in the Stedworth family and the only one to serve time. That was back before Uncle Ezra, one of Dad's other brothers and the former bank president, was sentenced to twenty years in the state pen for embezzlement.

"LeRoy moved to Nashville after his drive-thru combination porn shop and go-go bar went bust," said Dad. "He decided to become a country Western singer."

"I didn't know he could sing."

"He can't."

I sighed. "We need more clues."

"Jonah will lock you up and toss away the key if he catches you back at the motel," warned Mac.

Mom and Dad both stared at me. "Long story," I said. "Trust me, you don't want to know."

Dad started muttering again, something about how I wasn't like this before I moved to New York. I was tempted to ask him like what but thought better of it, especially when I caught the warning look Mac shot me, along with an almost imperceptible shake of his head.

"You're becoming a real party-pooping wuss," said Gertie.

Find your entertainment elsewhere, I told her.

"Like I have the power to become someone else's imaginary friend? Why don't you all head over to your mother's TV studio and snoop around for clues there?"

What good would that do us? Maude-Ann wasn't killed at the studio.

"You never know, but I'm not buying into this whole anonymous drugged-out burglar theory you've all got going."

45

Me neither. Besides, I kept coming back to that look exchanged between Phineas and Uncle Jonah yesterday.

If Maude-Ann spent several hours a day alone in Mom's office, maybe she left something behind that would point us in the direction of the killer. If nothing else, it would at least get us all out of the house. We certainly weren't accomplishing much sitting at the kitchen table, talking the situation around in circles.

SIX

Mom's TV studio was a converted barn, known for decades as The Big Red Barn. Years ago, it housed a flea market and country store run by a couple of long-deceased spinsters. I'm not sure how they were related to us, but Mom inherited the place back when I was six or seven. From time to time as I was growing up, Mom talked about turning The Big Red Barn into a combination antiques store/tearoom, but she either never found the time or the money or both. Back then, her life revolved around Dad and me and left little time for much else besides her various crafting projects and canning her blue-ribbon pickled beets. So The Big Red Barn, which was located just down the road from the Ten Commandments Inn, remained boarded up for years.

Besides, everyone in Ten Commandments already owned a houseful of antiques, because no one ever threw anything out. And who would pay for tea they could brew themselves in their own kitchen?

Within a matter of days after returning from her life-altering trip to New York, Mom found both the time and the money to transform The Big Red Barn into a television studio and headquarters for Connie Stedworth Enterprises. It's amazing what instant fame and the backing of an entrepreneurial Svengali can accomplish.

We all bundled up in mittens, mufflers, parkas, and boots, then piled into Dad's Tahoe for the short ride to The Big Red Barn.

Someone had beaten us to it.

The show was on hiatus over the holidays, production closed down until after New Year's. Yet the snow showed evidence of someone having traipsed around the perimeter of the place. The intermittent snowfalls, as well as the gusting winds, of the last few days made it difficult to tell just how *many* someones, but it was obvious that at least one person had been skulking around The Big Red Barn recently.

"Maybe one of the Shakelmeyer hogs got loose," I said. The Shakelmeyer hogs always made for convenient scapegoats. Or maybe that should be *scapepigs*.

"Not unless Porky wielded a crowbar," said Mac. "It looks like someone tried to break in." He pointed to gouges on the exterior façade around the doorframe.

"Wonderful," said Mom. She clapped her mittened hands together. "We've just been handed our first break in the case."

Mac swung his attention from the gouges to Mom. "How?"

Mom keyed in the code to release the lock on the state-of-the-art door that was far from a typical barn door. It swung open, and she stepped inside. "Come see."

She deactivated the alarm, then flipped on some lights and ushered us toward her office, one of three sectioned off directly to the left of the entry and situated behind a counter that served as a reception area. Mom's name was decoratively stenciled on the first door, Dad's on the second, and Mom's guru and partner, Hyman Perth, the man responsible for all things Connie Stedworth, on the third door. Three guesses who did the stenciling.

Mom opened her office door and headed to one of two desks in the room. She removed her mittens and booted up the computer. While the computer ran through the start-up sequence, she stripped off the rest of her outerwear and switched on the zoned heating in the room before settling down behind her desk.

"With all the expensive equipment we use for taping the show," she said, directing her comments to me, "your father and Hy both insisted on state-of-the-art security to protect our investment."

"This might look like an old barn from the outside," said Dad, "but it's as secure as Fort Knox. We have twenty-four-hour digital surveillance that feeds to a remote monitoring station accessible from any computer with an Internet connection."

The rest of us shed our outer layers and positioned ourselves behind Mom as she double-clicked on an icon that brought up a window requesting Username and Password. She entered both, typing so quickly that it was impossible to make out either before she hit the Enter key. Then she sat back and folded her arms across her chest as we all stared at a series of six screens, one for each camera positioned on The Big Red Barn.

"No one gets within a hundred yards of this place without being recorded," said Dad.

I noted the pride in his voice and stared in awe as my mother manipulated the computer keys. And to think at one time I believed my parents would have to be yanked kicking and screaming into the twenty-first century. Ever since Mom showed up unannounced on my Greenwich Village doorstep nearly two years ago, my parents had been surprising the hell out of me.

Mom reversed the recording to where one of the screens showed us first pulling up in the Tahoe. We watched ourselves exit the SUV, check out the disrupted snow and the building, then enter through the main door.

"So let's see who was nosing around the last few days," said Dad. "Start with when everyone left for the holidays, Connie."

Mom made a few clicks of the mouse, and we watched in triple-time as people streamed out of the building, made their way to various cars in the parking lot, and drove off. Mom, Dad, and Maude-Ann were the last to leave. After the three of them drove away, the parking lot was empty.

"When was this?" I asked.

"December twenty-second," said Mom. "The day before you and Mac arrived. I finished editing the last show we taped, then threw a Christmas party for the staff and crew."

"*You* do the editing?" I still couldn't wrap my head around the fact that my mother now had a *staff* and *crew*, let alone that she knew how to edit video.

"I work with an editor, but I have the final say," said Mom. "It *is* my show."

Right. *Her show.* One day my mother is pickling beets and stenciling cows above the kitchen chair rail; the next day she's CEO of a multi-million dollar media empire with a cable show, a bi-monthly magazine, craft and decorating books, and a line of assorted gift products. I felt like a slacker in comparison.

"Had everyone else already gone for the day?" asked Mac, getting us back to the reason we were all here.

Dad nodded. "We were the last to leave. No one else knows the security codes to lock up."

"What about Maude-Ann?" I asked.

"No, just your mother and me. And the security company, of course."

"And Hy," added Mom. "But he hasn't been here in over a month." She fast-forwarded the recording until the camera captured a patrol car pulling into the parking lot.

"Is that the sheriff?" asked Mac.

"Jonah," said Dad. "What's he doing there?"

We watched as Uncle Jonah checked the doors and windows around The Big Red Barn before getting back in his patrol car and driving off. "That was odd," I said. "What day was that?"

Mom checked the time stamp. "Yesterday. Right before he arrived for Christmas dinner. He didn't mention he'd been out checking the place."

"He also didn't mention that someone had ransacked Maude-Ann's apartment. Mac and I discovered that for ourselves this morning."

"Not so odd when you think about it," said Mac. "He already knew that someone tossed the place. If the killer didn't find what he was looking for, he may have figured Maude-Ann hid it somewhere else—like where she worked."

"So Jonah went to check on The Big Red Barn," said Dad. "Makes perfect sense."

Dad sounded relieved. I think we'd all been holding our collective breaths, waiting to see if Uncle Jonah took a crowbar to the door.

Mom continued to fast forward. No Shakelmeyer hogs popped up on the surveillance tapes, but as Christmas day waned and grew dark, a shadowy figure skulked into view. And he was definitely carrying a crowbar.

Mom froze the picture. "Who is that?"

We all squinted at the screen, but we couldn't even tell if the person was a man or a woman, let alone identify the would-be burglar. He looked more like the Michelin man the way he was bundled head to toe. A ski mask covered his face; a furry hood covered his head. We watched for several minutes as he tried to pry the door open, then left when his efforts proved in vain.

"Someone sure wants something he thinks Maude-Ann had," I said.

"Enough to kill for," added Mac.

"But what?" asked Mom. "Trust me. I knew the woman her entire life. She didn't own anything of value. No jewelry. No silver. Nothing."

"She must have had something," said Dad. "At least of value to the killer. We should start searching this place. Maybe she did hide something here."

I glanced around the room. Mom's office was a study in organized chaos, reminiscent of what our house used to look like whenever she was in one of her crafting frenzies. To the uninitiated it appeared to be a giant mess, but Mom always knew exactly where to find whatever she needed, down to the tiniest pompom or most miniscule google eye.

Whatever we were looking for could be hiding in plain sight and we'd never find it. And that was just the office. "The object of the killer's desire might be hidden anywhere in The Big Red Barn," I said. "And since we don't know what we're looking for, how do we go about finding it?"

"Maude-Ann kept to the office mostly," said Mom. She pointed across the room to the other desk. "She sat there."

"Then that's where we start." I crossed the room, pulled open the top desk drawer, and started rifling through it. "Assorted office stuff. Paper clips. Post-It notes. Pens. Pencils. A flash drive. A roll of masking tape." I slammed the drawer shut. The other draws proved equally bland. God forbid it should be that easy.

"It looks like we're going to be here for a while," said Mom.

~*~

We spent the next hour searching every nook and cranny of Mom's office but found nothing that didn't belong. "Maude-Ann never went anywhere else in the building?" I asked. "Maybe to get you something from the supply room? A cup of coffee from the break room? She at least went to the bathroom occasionally, right?"

Mom agreed that those were all possibilities. So we searched the supply room, the break room, and even the ladies' restroom. For three hours we poked in, around, under, and over anything that might contain Maude-Ann's mysterious Maltese Falcon. We turned up zip.

~*~

After three frustrating hours I sank into one of the semi-comfy chairs across from the reception counter and declared defeat. "Maybe the killer was after something that never existed," I said.

"Like what?" asked Mom.

I shrugged. "I don't know. But let's look at this from a different angle. Suppose he was some trucker who took a wrong turn off the interstate last week and wound up at a bar in Badger Bluffs. He's sitting nursing a beer and overhears a drunken conversation about this crazy old lady who owns the motel in Ten Commandments. He figures she's a rich recluse and easy pickings. So he waits until most people won't be out and about, then poses as a traveler needing a room for the night."

"But somehow things go terrible wrong," said Mom.

"Right. And Maude-Ann winds up dead instead of just robbed."

"You're both forgetting a few things," said Mac. He dropped down into the chair next to me, and we all turned to him. "Aside from the fact that the killer would have no reason to move the body to one of the motel rooms, whoever we saw on the surveillance tape came by foot. He didn't drive up in a truck or anything else. And how would this phantom trucker know anything about The Big Red Barn?"

"So much for that theory, Sherlock."

I don't hear any brilliant ideas coming from you, I told Gertie.

I wasn't giving up so easily. "What if the people in the bar were some of Mom's employees? They may have been talking about work and somehow the conversation drifted into discussing Maude-Ann."

"Seems like a long leap," said Mac.

"Not at all," I said. "She's always been a source of speculation, even back when I was a kid. Everyone used to talk about Maude-Ann like she was Miss Havisham or something."

"That still doesn't explain why the body was moved," said Dad.

I had an explanation for that, as well. "Maybe he decided to spend the night, and Maude-Ann's apartment was more comfortable than one of the guest rooms. She had food in the fridge and a better TV. He didn't want to share the place with a dead body, so he moved it to one of the motel rooms."

"Why so far, though?" asked Mom.

I threw my arms up in frustration. "I don't know! Maybe dead people give him the willies, and he wanted her as far away from him as possible. Maybe he believes in ghosts and figured she'd haunt the closest person, which would have been Mac."

"And the guy with the crowbar and no vehicle?" asked Mac.

I shrugged. "Someone else? We never did finish watching the tapes. How do we know there weren't other people lurking around The Big Red Barn the last few days? Maybe there's no connection between Maude-Ann's murder and the attempted break-in."

So we all headed back into Mom's office to scan through the remainder of the surveillance tape. This time we did see one of the Shakelmeyer hogs heading toward The Big Red Barn in the wee hours of this morning. The beast was followed a few frames later by Leona Shakelmeyer. Only Leona didn't appear to be chasing after a runaway porker.

"It looks like she's herding the hog right toward the barn," said Mac. "Why would she do that?"

Mom paused the recording. "Leona's always snooping around. The woman's been competing against me and coming up short her entire life. She even tried to steal Earnest from me back in high school. Asked him to the Sadie Hawkins Day dance when I was laid up with chicken pox. She knew Earnest and I were practically engaged, but that didn't stop her."

Dad put his arm around Mom's shoulders and kissed her cheek. "You know I'd never look twice at Leona Shakelmeyer or anyone else, dear."

"Now," said Mom. "Back then I was younger and insecure."

I glanced up at Mac. Would we still be that much in love when we were in our fifties? He laced his fingers through mine and gave my hand a squeeze, as if assuring me I had nothing to worry about.

"I don't know what Leona could possibly expect to find

skulking around here," said Dad. "The place was locked tight."

"Leona is too filled with bitterness to think straight half the time," said Mom. "I gave up a long time ago trying to understand that woman. Even when she gets what she wants, she's not satisfied. Like when she orchestrated that campaign to have Ralph replace you as mayor."

Mom clicked the mouse to advance the screen. The four of us watched as Leona looked around, apparently to make sure no one saw her. Then she pulled off her glove, removed a scrap of paper from her coat pocket, and proceeded to fiddle with the keypad.

"She's trying to break in!" cried Mom.

We continued watching as Leona grew more and more frustrated. Finally, she shoved the paper back in her pocket and gave the door a swift kick of her boot. Then she stormed off, leaving the hog to find his own way home.

"What do you think she was after?" I asked.

"Knowing Leona, probably nothing," said Dad. "She most likely only wanted to snoop around."

"That woman is too curious for her own good," said Mom. "I should have her arrested for attempting to break in. We've got her red-handed."

"Curiosity killed the cat," said Gertie.

But not Maude-Ann, I told her. *What possible motive would Leona Shakelmeyer have to kill Maude-Ann Krissendorf?*

"Who knows what evil lurks in the minds of the Shakelmeyers?"

Although…"Maybe the guy with the crow bar wasn't a guy," I said. "Maybe he was a she."

"And maybe she thought she could just pry open the door," said Mac. "When that failed, she came back with what she thought were the most likely codes you'd use. Birthdays. Anniversary. That sort of thing."

Mom snorted. "How stupid does she think we are?"

No one had time to comment, though, because just then we heard a car pull uutside. A moment later, the door swung open.

SEVEN

"Earnest, you here?" yelled Uncle Jonah.

Dad moved to the door, pulling it behind him as he stepped out of the office. "What's up, Jonah?"

Mom quickly exited out of the surveillance program. "Not that I don't trust him," she muttered under her breath.

Mac and I shared a meaningful look. I don't think any of us trusted Uncle Jonah much anymore, but was he capable of murder? And if so, what reason could he have for killing Maude-Ann?

The three of us crept across the room and hovered near the door, listening as Uncle Jonah answered Dad. "I was wondering if you'd mind me taking a look at Maude-Ann's computer, Earnest."

"The one she used here at work?" asked Dad. "What on earth for?"

Uncle Jonah cleared his throat. "I know it's probably a long shot, but maybe I can find a lead by seeing where she'd been and what she'd been up to online."

"Hmm...I suppose you have to be careful about those crafting chat rooms she monitored for Connie. You never know about those scrapbooking enthusiasts and die-hard decoupagers."

"So that's where you get your sarcasm gene," said Gertie.

Who would have guessed? Sometimes I wondered if my parents were abducted by aliens at some point because they sure weren't the same people I'd known before I left Ten Commandments for Manhattan.

Uncle Jonah's voice grew testy. "Don't be dense, Earnest. The woman was a loner, and loners tend to get themselves mixed up with cyberspace creeps. For all we know, she could have pretended she was a twenty-year-old blonde and spent her nights having cybersex with a host of losers from California to Calcutta."

"Don't you need a warrant or something?" asked Dad. "You know, to make it legal in court."

"Not if you willingly give me the computer," said Uncle Jonah. "I can get one if I have to. I just thought maybe you'd be willing to save us all a lot of time and trouble by handing over the computer."

Mom tiptoed back to her desk and pulled open the bottom drawer. She lifted out a laptop and headed back toward us.

"What about not trusting Uncle Jonah?" I whispered as she was about to open the office door.

She shushed me and whispered back, "I don't." Then she opened the door and stepped out into the reception area. "What a great idea, Jonah. Here. Let us know if we can be of further assistance."

"Why, thank you, Connie. I'll definitely do that."

Just as quickly as he came, Uncle Jonah was out the door and starting up the engine of his police cruiser.

"Why'd you give him the computer?" I asked Mom as she and Dad returned to the office.

"Trust me," she said. "He won't find anything of interest on that laptop. Just old files of craft designs and show schedules. I was only holding on to it for spare parts. Maude-Ann didn't even know it was here." She stepped over to Maude-Ann's desk and scooped up the laptop sitting on it. "We're taking this baby home with us to see what Jonah's so eager to find."

"And the plot thickens," said Gertie.

We donned our winter gear and were about to leave when something occurred to me. "Wait," I said, dashing back into Mom's office. I opened Maude-Ann's desk drawer and pocketed the flash drive I'd seen earlier. Whatever Uncle Jonah was looking for might be stored on the drive and not the laptop.

~*~

After we ate a quick lunch of Christmas leftovers, we gathered around Maude-Ann's work laptop and began searching through the files for anything that might be a motive for murder. But after an hour of clicking on one file after another, we'd exhausted all the folders on the desktop and come up with zilch.

"Maybe we'll have better luck with the flash drive," I said. I pulled off the cap and was about to insert it into one of the ports when Mac placed his hand over mine.

"Hold off on that for a minute. Let's see if there are any additional files not on the desktop."

That's when we found them.

"Whoa!" said Mac, accessing the first of several dozen videos.

"Oh. My. God." I stared at the moving images on the screen, not believing what my eyes were seeing. "Another day, another sex scandal in good old Ten Commandments."

"That's enough!" Mom slammed the laptop lid so fast and so hard that she nearly guillotined Mac's fingers.

Dad lifted the lid back up, clicked out of the first video, and opened the next. "We have to search through all the files, Connie. This is most likely the reason someone killed Maude-Ann."

"Then you do it. Just do it without me." Mom stormed out of the kitchen. I'm not sure whether she was angry, hurt, or embarrassed by what she'd seen. Maybe a combination of all three.

Maude-Ann apparently led a secret life that she kept from the cousin who had always cared about her, yet not from many town's people who had never shown her much in the way of kindness or respect. Then again, maybe what we were viewing was the reason they didn't show her any kindness or respect in public. They were certainly showing her all sorts of other things in private. And to think, I'd assumed Maude-Ann was a dried-up virgin.

"Just goes to show you how looks can be deceiving," said Gertie. *And how!*

I glanced to my left, then my right, and took some comfort in the realization that I wasn't the only one embarrassed by the homemade porn. Mac looked more than slightly uncomfortable, and Dad looked positively mortified. I'm willing to bet this was Dad's first experience with porn of any kind. After all, my father was Jim Anderson, Ward Cleaver, and Ozzie Nelson all rolled up into one. I doubt he'd ever even flipped through a copy of *Playboy* or *Penthouse*—just for the articles, mind you—not to mention *Hustler*. And what we were viewing definitely out-hustled *Hustler*.

With mounting displeasure Dad, Mac, and I continued to search through the files one by one. We had no choice if we were going to figure out who killed Maude-Ann.

Each file was labeled by date and the initials of Maude-Ann's co-star. The dates went back several years. This was no mid-life crisis, no manifestation of a life altering epiphany that struck with the onset of menopause and caused Maude-Ann to experience life before it was too late. Maude-Ann was ten years younger than Mom. That made her only forty-two when she died and only thirty-seven at the time the first escapade on the computer was recorded. There was no way of knowing if her kinky life pre-dated the first recording, and if so, by how long.

Living in New York had opened my mind to many alternative lifestyles. I never passed judgment. I believed in a creed of live-and-let-live. But this was Ten Commandments, Iowa, and some of these dudes getting it on in very weird ways were my former schoolteachers, not to mention church elders and other bastions of the god-fearing, law-abiding community where I was born and raised.

I clicked out of a video that featured my old high school principal—definitely a TMI moment if ever there was one—and was about to click on the next file when I noticed the initials in the file name. I hesitated, afraid to click. "Dad?"

"Nori!" His already crimson face darkened several shades deeper. I hoped he'd taken his blood pressure meds this morning. But instead of anger, I heard disappointment in his voice. "How could you even think such a thing?"

"Sorry, Dad, but when even Phineas Draymore—"

"Let's keep that particular piece of knowledge to ourselves. Your mother doesn't need to know her best friend's husband committed adultery with her cousin. As for me..." Dad reached across the keyboard and clicked the mouse. Up popped Elias Sunderson in his birthday suit, an image I could have lived the rest of my life without seeing. I should have known not to worry about

Dad. He'd be the last upstanding guy standing in Ten Commandments come Judgment Day.

"All this proves is that Maude-Ann had a very active and...uhm...imaginative sex life," said Mac.

"Imaginative?" said Gertie. *"Interesting euphemism. Try kinky."*

Try extremely kinky. Who knew there were so many fetishists living in Ten Commandments, Iowa?

"But why record herself having sex with all these guys?" I asked. "What happens in the bedroom should stay in the bedroom. Especially this kind of stuff. Memories can't wind up on YouTube."

"Maybe that's it," said Mac. "Let's look at that flash drive now. I'm willing to bet I know what's on it, and it goes back to something you suggested earlier, Nori."

I slipped the flash drive into one of the ports on the side of the computer. It contained one file, a spreadsheet. The left column contained the video file names. Then there were a series of additional columns filled with numbers. "It looks like a page from an accounting ledger," I said.

"Blackmail records?" asked Dad.

"I thinks so," said Mac. "The first column would indicate the guy and the date of the video. The other columns appear to be progressive dates, all within a few days of each other but quite some time after the videos were made, often a few years. They could be the date she first contacted the guy, the date he responded to her demand, and the date he made the initial payment."

"And the other columns indicate the dates and amounts paid," I said. "Looks like Maude-Ann had them all on a once-a-month payment schedule."

"Talk about a lucrative revenue stream," said Dad. "All of these men would pay through the nose to keep those videos away from their wives."

"Until someone got fed up with paying and found a permanent solution to his problem," I said.

"Well, we've certainly increased our list of potential suspects," said Mac.

"And discovered what Uncle Jonah wanted to keep secret," I added. "No wonder he got all bent out of shape when anyone suggested calling in the state to investigate the murder. These videos are both marriage killers and career killers."

"Don't forget Maude-Ann killers," said Gertie.

Not that anyone could after what we'd viewed.

~*~

In all, there were twelve Ten Commandments perverts being blackmailed by Maude-Ann. We compiled a list of names before shutting down the computer. Then we called Mom back into the kitchen and explained what we'd discovered, minus any mention of Phineas Draymore.

"What is it with men?" she asked, directing her question to Dad and Mac.

Mac held his hands up. "Hey, don't shoot the messenger. There's already been too much gunfire in this town."

Dad looked offended. "I don't understand this any more than you do, dear."

"I can assure you the entire male population doesn't engage in deviant behavior," added Mac.

"Besides," I said. "We need to concentrate on what's important right now—outing the killer. We now have a motive, but we still don't know who pulled the trigger."

"One thing I'll say about Maude-Ann," said Dad. "She certainly wasn't Madoff greedy, demanding only three grand a year from each man."

"Just enough to feather a little tax-free retirement nest egg," said Mom. "It just never occurred to me that she was feathering it on her back."

I tried to suppress a giggle and failed miserably.

Mom glared. "I don't see the humor in this, Nori."

I did. "From what we saw, Mom, Maude-Ann was rarely on her back."

Mom covered her ears with her hands, closed her eyes, and shook her head. "Enough! I don't want details."

"What doesn't make sense to me," said Dad, "is that anyone would kill over three thousand dollars a year. I know these men. They blow more than that each year on the riverboat casinos."

"All of them?" I asked.

Dad scanned the list of names again. "Well, almost all."

That's when I knew who killed Maude-Ann. And it wasn't Uncle Jonah.

EIGHT

"Now all we have to do is trick the murderer into confessing," I told Mom, Dad, and Mac.

"I hope you've got that figured out, as well," said Mac.

"Without putting us in any danger," added Mom.

But how?

"Do I have to do everything around here?" asked Gertie. *"With the old con-the-con routine, of course."*

Hey, an actual suggestion! And with minimal snark. Was my imaginary friend finally beginning to lose her 'tude?

"Never. I'm just getting bored with all this Sherlock Holmes wannabe crap. Let's wrap it up already."

Ah, now that's the Gertie I know and love.

Still, I had to admit her suggestion was brilliant. No matter how often the cops execute that particular sting in New York, greedy deadbeat dads, tax scofflaws, and other assorted pond scum continue to fall for it. Why shouldn't it work in Ten Commandments?

I laid out the bare bones of my plan, hoping a little brainstorming would flesh out the details. "First, we need a reason to bring all these men together at the same place and at the same time. The best way to do that is to offer them something they want."

Mac smiled at me. "Genius! I see exactly where you're going."

"I'm afraid I don't," said Mom.

"I'm beginning to," said Dad. He gave Mom's hand a squeeze. "It will become clear to you in a minute, dear."

"When the cops pull this scam in the city," said Mac, "they often use the lure of a sweepstakes win. I'm not sure that's going to work in Ten Commandments, though."

"I know. If any of these guys entered a sweepstakes, they'd remember. We need something they'll fall for without question." I turned to Dad. "Can you think of anything? Something they all have in common—other than the obvious, of course—."

"Why not the obvious?" asked Mac. "They're all into kinky sex, and they were all being blackmailed by Maude-Ann. How did they find out about her little enterprise?"

"Well, she certainly wasn't advertising in the church bulletin," said Mom.

"No, but she had to be advertising somewhere," said Dad. "Someplace where she could keep her identity secret."

"There's only one place to do that," said Mac. "The Internet." He flipped open the laptop and started searching through the browser history.

I read down the list that popped up. "DMCUSA dot com, DecoArt dot com, Coats and Clark dot com—"

"Craft companies," said Mom. "Most of Maude-Ann's job was to act as a liaison between the show and the companies whose products we featured, so we didn't get nasty letters from frustrated consumers when they couldn't find products they needed to make a particular project. We package kits they can purchase directly from us."

More than anyone needed to know. I nodded at Mom and continued to read. "Kreinik dot com, Sudberry dot com, Fantasy Craft dot com, Amos Craft dot com—"

"Wait!" said Mom.

"Amos Craft?" I asked.

"No, the one before that. Fantasy Craft. There's no such company. At least not that I know of."

And if anyone would know every craft company in the country, it was Connie Stedworth, the Queen of Crafts. Mac clicked on the URL for Fantasy Craft.

"Bingo!" he said as soon as the site loaded. Fantasy Craft was definitely no manufacturer of pompoms or embroidery floss. Mac did a *Whois* search, and the address for the Ten Commandments Inn popped up.

"Maude-Ann probably advertised the website on sites that catered to a certain segment of society," said Dad. "Once she connected with someone on the 'net, she made arrangements to connect in person."

"But don't you think it's odd that only men in Ten Commandments got in touch with her?" asked Mom.

"We don't know that," I said. "Unless we can dig up other records, we may never know how many guys she...uhm...er—" I knew the word I wanted to use, but I wasn't going to use it in front of my parents. They'd had enough shocks for one day.

"Serviced?" supplied Mac.

"That'll do," I said, offering him a grateful smile. "*Serviced.*

Anyway, it doesn't mean she didn't...uhm...*service* others and charge them an hourly rate. Once a trucker or two booked a room, the word probably spread. She may only have been blackmailing men she knew. Men she felt safe would pay up and not harm her or go to the police."

"Until one of them did harm her," said Mom. "You think you know someone..." Her voice trailed off, and she got this really perplexed look on her face. "But why would she use the office computer and not her personal one? This side business of hers started long before Connie Stedworth Enterprises existed."

"She probably did at first," said Mac. "But once you hired her, it was safer for her to keep everything on one of the company computers. She knew the chance of you or Earnest finding the videos was highly unlikely. So The Big Red Barn became a giant safety deposit box of sorts. As long as none of her marks worked here, there was little chance of any of them getting hold of the videos."

"I suppose it all makes sense," said Mom. "But how are we going to trap the killer?"

"Simple," I said. "We invite all twelve men to a party."

~*~

Coming up with something that would guarantee these twelve men showed up took a bit of brainstorming. We needed something exclusive, something where they wouldn't bring friends or spouses, nor talk about the event to anyone else. Each man had to believe he was singled out for something special, something that didn't raise any suspicions and was as far removed from blackmail and murder as possible.

"I'll bet these guys are going nuts, wondering if those videos were destroyed in the fire or if they'll show up somewhere," I said.

"I wonder if they know about each other," said Mac. "What's the likelihood of that?" he asked, directing his question to Dad.

"What? That they discussed their predilection for...for..."

Poor Dad. His face reddened. He couldn't even say it.

"Alternative recreation?" I supplied.

He nodded his thanks to me and continued, "It's certainly not a topic that ever came up at the Grange Hall or anywhere else when I was present."

Not that this helped at all. As I've previously mentioned, Dad was the personification of the nineteen-fifties sit-com father come to life. I'll bet half the town thought my parents slept in twin beds. Talk about sex—even non-adulterous, mission style-only sex—in front of my Dad? I guarantee that's the day there'd be blizzards in Hell.

"At least two of them know about each other," I said. One particular video explained the worried exchange between Uncle Jonah and Phineas Draymore the day of the fire.

"I have an idea," said Mom. "We invite them all to a special event at The Big Red Barn."

"Mom, I don't see any of these guys picking up knitting needles or decoupage brushes any time soon."

"They won't be knitting or decoupaging," she said. "They'll be invited to a special dinner for the purpose of market research."

"And why will they bother to show up?" asked Mac.

"Because we'll entice them with lots of freebies."

"Again, Mom, free craft supplies for perverts?"

Mom sighed one of her why-are-you-so-dense-sometimes? sighs. "No, Nori, not craft supplies. Free stuff all men want."

"Like?"

She thought for a moment. "How about an all-expense paid

trip for two to Chicago with tickets to a football game or some other sporting event? You know, Bears, Bulls, Cubs, Sox—whatever. But that might not be enough." She grew silent for another moment, then added, "And a chance to win a brand-new truck. That will really bring them running. But they have to be present to win. Of course, they really won't be receiving anything other than the shock of their lives. Although I suppose I will need to cook something so the place is filled with drool-worthy aromas."

"Free food. Free trip. Free wheels. That should guarantee they'll all show," said Dad.

"Throw in free booze," suggested Gertie.

Good one. "Plus, an open bar," I said.

"But what about Jonah?" asked Dad. "Do we tell him what's really going on?"

"No, we can't do that," I said. "There's still the chance I'm wrong about this, and he's our killer."

"Jonah is obviously capable of all sorts of unsavory things," said Dad, "but I don't believe he'd ever kill anyone."

"You're probably right, Dad, but he's still got to remain as clueless as the rest of the men since he's on the videos."

"We have to contact some authority, though," said Mac. "Someone who can make an arrest."

"Earnest, you should give Cliff Tuttle a call," said Mom.

"Of course," said Dad. "I should have thought to call him the moment Jonah refused to contact the Department of Criminal Investigations."

"Who's Cliff Tuttle?" I asked.

"He's the county district attorney," said Mom, "but more importantly, he's your father's old college roommate."

~*~

Cliff Tuttle came running. According to Dad, the county D.A. had grand plans for himself. Having his name linked with orchestrating a sting that caught a murderer would go a long way in his bid to become the next junior congressman from the great state of Iowa. The guy actually thanked us for calling *him*!

A couple of hours later, the five of us were well on our way toward creating a sting operation, the first in the county's history. Our initial order of business was designing an appropriate invitation to entice our twelve suspects. With input from Mom, Mac and I came up with the perfect lure.

Connie Stedworth Enterprises cordially invites you to a
Guys' Night Out
Tomorrow evening, 6pm at The Big Red Barn

This is an invitation-only event to a select group of men whose opinions we value. In exchange for a few minutes of market research you'll receive:

A five-course prime rib dinner with open bar
An all-expense paid trip for two to Chicago
Two tickets to the Chicago sporting event of your choice
The chance to win a brand new Chevy Silverado

Once we printed out the invitations, Mac and I left to hand-delivering them while Mom, Dad, and Cliff took care of all the other details. Operation CAMP (Catch a Murdering Pervert) was officially underway.

~*~

By five-forty the following evening all twelve men had arrived. I guess they wanted to get an early start on sampling the wares of the open bar. Mac and I ushered them inside one by one, taking their coats, and showing them to the conference room, a section of The Big Red Barn directly across the main entryway from the reception area and offices. No one acted the least bit suspicious from what we could tell, just lots of backslapping and congratulating of each other for being singled out to receive some damn fine swag—my word, not theirs.

"These bozos wouldn't know swag from a Venetian blind," said Gertie.

True. But the sentiment remained the same. As they downed beer after beer, they bragged to each other about how much Mom valued their opinions and how vital they were to the success of Connie Stedworth Enterprises. It took Herculean will-power on my part to bite my tongue, smile, and keep my eyes from rolling as I refilled beer steins from the keg Mom and Dad had purchased for the occasion.

At six-ten Mac and I had the men take their seats. "Before we serve dinner," I said, "we're going to show you a series of videos. Please direct your attention to the television monitor at the far end of the room."

"Can't we watch while we eat?" asked Phineas Draymore.

"Afraid not," I said.

"What are you making us watch, Nori? Ain't no infomercials on making little do-dads, is it?" asked Elias Sunderson.

"No, I think you'll find this much more interesting than an infomercial."

"Good," he said, "because I'm not interested in no do-dads. Maybe our wives are but not us, right fellas?"

They all voiced agreement.

"The sooner we get started," said Mac, "the sooner we can serve dinner. I'm sure you can all smell that prime rib Connie cooked up for you."

At that, the twelve men shifted their chairs, so their backs faced me. "Everyone ready?" I asked.

"Hell, yes," said Uncle Jonah. "Let's get the show on the road so we can dig into that prime rib dinner you promised us."

"And find out who wins the Silverado," added Ralph Shakelmeyer.

Mac switched off the lights, plunging the room into total darkness. I reached behind me and turned the doorknob, the signal for Cliff Tuttle and several officers from the state Department of Criminal Investigations to slip unseen into the room.

"Enjoy the show, gentlemen." I pressed the remote, and the first images filled the fifty-four-inch flat screen mounted on the wall.

Mac had spliced together a montage from the various videos on Maude-Ann's computer. Each man appeared with Maude-Ann for only ten seconds. But ten seconds of naked, overweight middle-aged men doing what these guys were doing was more than enough.

I wasn't sure what to expect the moment our neighborhood pervs were confronted with the proof of their deviant deeds, but absolute you-could-hear-a-pin-drop silence hadn't even made my Top Ten List. I wasn't even sure they were all still breathing. No one uttered a syllable, let alone a groan or gasp or angry stream of four-letter words.

"Maybe they all dropped dead," said Gertie.

No, as I positioned myself at the side of the room and my eyes adjusted to the dim light of the television screen, I saw that every single one of them sat rigid, hands grasping chair arms to the point their white knuckles stood out in the darkness. Their mouths open, jaws dropped, eyes bulging, one by one they recognized not only themselves but each other, and the implications sunk in.

At the end of the two-minute show, Cliff flipped the lights back on. Slowly, the men turned to face the front of the room. When they saw Cliff and his officers, guns drawn, barring the door, all hell broke loose.

"I didn't kill her!"

"I have an alibi!"

"You're not pinning this on me!"

"I want a lawyer!"

"I didn't do nothing to her!"

Voices rose to be heard over each other, purple veins throbbing along the sides of red-faced men, growing angrier and angrier. Except for one. One man still sat at the table, his hands folded in front of him, his head bowed, his lips moving. He finished praying and raised his head. His face had turned a sickly yellow-green, and sweat glistened along his brow. Ralph Shakelmeyer turned toward Cliff Tuttle and said, "I didn't do it, but I know who did. I want a deal."

NINE

Cliff Tuttle joined us for a prime rib dinner back at the house later that evening. As we ate, he filled us in on what had transpired after all twelve men were carted off for questioning and Mom, Dad, Mac, and I had gone home. "Would you believe some of them actually complained about not getting those goodies they were promised?" he said.

"What's going to happen to them?" I asked.

"Nothing as far as the state is concerned. The sex was consensual, and the blackmailer's dead. Stupidity isn't a crime, not even in Iowa." He shook his head and chuckled. "I sure as hell wouldn't want to be in their shoes when the story hits the news wires, though."

Mac chuckled right along with him. "Everyone loves to read about a good sex scandal," he said.

"And in an upstanding Midwest town called Ten Commandments?" added Cliff. "Brace yourselves for the paparazzi."

Dad groaned.

"Could be worse," I said. "At least you're no longer the mayor, and Uncle Jonah didn't have anything to do with Maude-Ann's murder."

From the expression on his face, I don't think he took much comfort from either fact. Ten Commandments would never be the same. Deep down inside, I believe Dad would like nothing better than to have life go back to the way it was long before Mom's visit to New York changed the world as he knew it. Now it had once again shifted on its axis, and poor Dad was having trouble keeping up.

"You can't always get what you want," sing-songed Gertie.

But then there's Karma, I told her.

"Yeah," she agreed. *"And in this case, it's a real bitch."*

I had figured Ralph Shakelmeyer for the killer, because I knew the Shakelmeyers were even bigger tightwads than Maude-Ann. No way would Ralph ever spend an evening on a floating casino. I'd been wrong, though. Dead wrong. Not about the riverboat gambling but about Ralph killing Maude-Ann.

"Ralph Shakelmeyer sang like the proverbial canary," said Cliff. "Once he was promised a suspended sentence for his part in the cover-up."

"But I thought spouses couldn't testify against each other," I said.

"They can't be forced to testify against each other," said Mom, once again trumping me as the *Law & Order* expert of the family. "They can testify if they want to."

Cliff concurred. "And Ralph certainly wanted to testify to save his own hide."

Yes, Leona Shakelmeyer, the nastiest woman in all of Ten

Commandments and the bane of my mother's existence for most of her life, had killed Maude-Ann Krissendorf. Her grandchildren would be having grandchildren before she ever saw them again—if she lived that long.

"According to Ralph," explained Cliff. "Leona was the kind of woman who could account for every pig farming penny she and Ralph had ever made."

"No secret there," said Mom. "Anyone in Ten Commandments could have told you that."

"I suppose so," said Cliff. "Anyway, things weren't adding up to her satisfaction. Money was missing, and she couldn't figure out where it was going.

"Leona began snooping around and eventually discovered that Ralph was siphoning money to pay Maude-Ann every month. When she confronted Ralph, he broke down and confessed to having an affair with Maude-Ann a few years ago and that she'd been blackmailing him ever since. Leona was only interested in getting back the money. So she confronted Maude-Ann and demanded the return of everything Ralph had paid her over the years—with interest."

"Typical," said Mom.

"Maybe Maude-Ann would have paid to keep Leona quiet, but Leona was too greedy," continued Cliff.

"Unlikely," I said. "Maude-Ann was so cheap, she locked the guest room thermostats. I can't see her paying Leona anything."

"And Leona being Leona, I'll bet she tried to bleed Maude-Ann," said Mom.

"Exactly," said Cliff. "According to Ralph, Leona tried to turn the tables on Maude-Ann, blackmailing the blackmailer."

"But why did she shoot her?" I asked. "She wouldn't get any

money from a dead body, and you said the money was all she cared about."

"Things got ugly," said Cliff. "You had a battle going between two tightwads. Neither was willing to give up a penny. Leona pulled a gun. There was a struggle, and the gun went off."

Cliff took a deep breath, then finished, "Leona claims it was an accident. We'll leave that for the jury to decide."

"And Ralph?" asked Mom. "What was his role in Maude-Ann's murder?"

"Leona panicked when she realized Maude-Ann was dead. She ran home and told Ralph what had happened. He told her he'd help, but he wanted the video. So while he moved the body, hoping to make it look like Maude-Ann was killed by some drifter who'd rented a room for the night, Leona tore apart Maude-Ann's apartment."

"Looking for the blackmail video."

"Right."

"But what about the explosion and fire?" asked Mac.

"That was Leona's doing," said Cliff. "According to Ralph, she couldn't stop worrying that they might have left incriminating evidence behind, especially if the video was hidden somewhere else around the motel. So she concocting an explosive device from some fertilizer, gasoline, and an alarm clock and slipped it into the room Christmas morning. The fire chief confirmed the fire was set by a rudimentary explosive device."

"Where in the world did Leona learn how to build a bomb?" asked Dad.

"Ralph said she found a 'recipe' on the Internet." Cliff turned to me and Mac. "You two must have just missed her when you arrived at the motel."

"She nearly killed us," I said.

"Attempted murder is one of the many crimes she's being charged with," said Cliff.

"But Ralph still didn't have the video," said Mom. "So that's why she tried to break into The Big Red Barn, figuring it might be there if it wasn't destroyed in the fire?"

"Exactly," said Cliff. "If someone else found that video, she and Ralph would be prime suspects. But she thought there was only one video—the one of Maude-Ann with Ralph. She still has no idea about the other men, the extent of the blackmail, or the kinky nature of the sex. If she doesn't plead out, it's going to be one very salacious trial."

Dad groaned again.

~*~

That night after Mom and Dad went to bed, Mac and I toasted marshmallows in front of the fireplace and pigged out on s'mores. "This certainly hasn't been the boring Christmas you warned me about," he said.

"Definitely not." I fashioned another s'more and fed it to him. "You know, I kind of liked playing Sherlock Holmes and outing the bad guys. If you ever fire me from my radio gig, I could become a P.I."

"I guess that means I'm never firing you."

"Besides, you didn't exactly solve anything," said my snarky imaginary friend. *"Ralph confessed and ratted out Leona."*

But who came up with the idea that set everything in motion?

Gertie mumbled a reluctant, *"You."*

Elementary, my dear Gertie.

A NOTE FROM THE AUTHOR

Dear Reader,

I hope you enjoyed *Elementary, My Dear Gertie*, the novella sequel to *Talk Gertie to Me*. If so, please consider leaving a review at your favorite review site.

If you like books that tickle your funny bone, you might also enjoy reading my two humorous amateur sleuth mystery series, the Anastasia Pollack Crafting Mysteries and the Empty Nest Mysteries, as well as my romantic comedy, *Hooking Mr. Right*, and my humorous women's fiction, *Four Uncles and a Wedding*. You can read about these books and others at my website, www.loiswinston.com, where you'll also find excerpts of each book as well as links for signing up for my newsletter and following me on various social media sites.

Happy reading!
Lois Winston

ABOUT THE AUTHOR

USA Today and Amazon bestselling and award-winning author Lois Winston writes mystery, romance, romantic suspense, chick lit, women's fiction, children's chapter books, and nonfiction. *Kirkus Reviews* dubbed her critically acclaimed Anastasia Pollack Crafting Mystery series, "North Jersey's more mature answer to Stephanie Plum." In addition, Lois is an award-winning craft and needlework designer who often draws much of her source material for both her characters and plots from her experiences in the crafts industry. Learn more about Lois and her books, where to find her on social media, and a link for signing up for her newsletter at www.loiswinston.com.